Ghost Rescue

AND THE
DINOSAURS

Ghost Rescue

AND THE DINOSAURS

WRITTEN BY
Andrew Murray

ILLUSTRATED BY
Sarah Horne

ORCHARD BOOKS

ORCHARD BOOKS
338 Euston Road, London NW1 3BH
Orchard Books Australia
Level 17/207 Kent Street, Sydney, NSW 2000
First published in hardback in Great Britain in 2008 by Orchard Books
First published in paperback in 2009
ISBN 978 1 84616 356 2 (hardback)
ISBN 978 1 84616 364 7 (paperback)
Text © Andrew Murray 2009
Illustrations © Sarah Horne 2009
The rights of Andrew Murray to be identified as the author and of
Sarah Horne to be identified as the illustrator of this work have been asserted by
them in accordance with the Copyright, Designs and Patents Act, 1988.
A CIP catalogue record for this book is available from the British Library.
1 3 5 7 9 10 8 6 4 2 (hardback)
1 3 5 7 9 10 8 6 4 2 (paperback)
Printed in Great Britain
Orchard Books is a division of Hachette Children's Books,
an Hachette UK company.
www.hachette.co.uk

A hundred years ago, an old grey man was hunched beneath a cliff searching for dinosaur fossils.

Gilbert Saxifrage was very small and very clever. He knew a lot about dinosaurs, and he knew a lot about fossils – bones that have turned to stone – and he also knew how dangerous it was to be hunched beneath a cliff.

He chipped at the rock with his little hammer – *chip, chip, chip…*

Suddenly a layer of rock fell away to reveal…

…"An allosaurus arm bone!" cried Gilbert. *"Hooray!"*

"Hooray-ay-ay-ay…" The sound echoed around the cliff. Gilbert looked up as a shadow appeared under the brim of his bowler hat. The shadow grew larger.

"Oh dear," said Gilbert Saxifrage.

A bowler hat is hard and strong – but not hard and strong enough to stop a two-tonne rock. And so, a hundred years ago, Gilbert Saxifrage became a ghost. *SPLAT!*

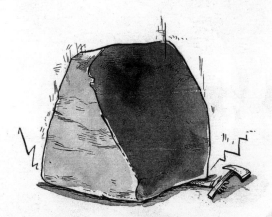

Gilbert's ghost had haunted the cliff ever since. He was kept company by the ghosts of all the dinosaurs whose bones had turned to stone in the cliff. Fierce tyrannosauruses, gentle brachiosauruses, flying pteranodons – they roared, and clawed, and stamped, but they were just ghosts, and they couldn't hurt Gilbert.

One night Gilbert saw a van drive up beside the cliff. It was old and rusty, and belching black smoke. Its sides were covered with paper and tape. Out of it climbed Arthur and Baz Crabtree. Arthur was much smaller than Baz, but he was the older brother and was clearly in charge. Arthur took out a pickaxe.

"Right, Baz," Arthur said. "You know what to do."

Baz grumbled as they picked their way over the fallen rocks to the cliff. "Why *me?*" he complained. "Why do I have to do the digging?"

"Baz," said Arthur, "you *know* I'd do it myself if I could, but I've got a bad leg. I wouldn't be able to dodge any falling rocks."

"Yes Arthur, I know..." sighed
Baz, as he swung the pickaxe into
the cliff. *Thwack-ack-ack!* The sound
echoed, and a stream of pebbles fell
on Baz's back.

"Arthur," said Baz, "couldn't I at least have a hard hat to wear?"

"*Baz*," said Arthur crossly, "do you know how much hard hats cost?"

"Yes, Arthur," sighed Baz. "Sorry, Arthur..."

Thwack-ack-ack! Thwack-ack-ack!

Gilbert's ghost watched as Baz dug deeper into the rock. "What *are* they up to?" he wondered.

He crept closer, and saw that Baz was digging out a fossilised dinosaur bone.

"The ankle of an ankylosaurus..." said Gilbert. "What are they going to—"

"*Look out!*" shrieked Baz. With a rumbling roar, a rock came loose above him. It came crashing down towards his head. But at the last moment the rock hit an outcrop, and bounced away from the cliff, tumbling straight towards—

"*Arthur! Look OUT!*"

With the speed of a circus acrobat, Arthur cartwheeled out of the way. The rock bounced clean over the van, and finally rolled to a stop. Arthur, Baz and even Gilbert's ghost breathed a deep sigh of relief.

"I thought you had a bad leg," said Baz.

"My leg?" said Arthur. "Oh, yes…my *leg*!" And he suddenly grabbed his knee and started to hobble. "Ow! Ow! *Owww!*"

Baz looked at his brother suspiciously, but he was more curious about the fossilised bone that he had cut free. "What kind of dinosaur was it from?" he asked.

"A BIG one," chuckled Arthur, "and that's all that matters! Come on, baby brother, let's put the bone in the van."

Naturally, Baz was the one who had to carry it. As he took the fossil further and further from the cliff, Baz looked back, Arthur looked back, and Gilbert looked back.

"*AAOUUWWRROOUUGH!*" An awful roar echoed around the cliff. And then it appeared – the great grey shape of a ghostly ankylosaurus, stomping its stumpy legs, swinging its club of a tail, and roaring in rage at the theft of its ankle.

"*AAOUUWWRROOUUGH!*"

"Hurry!" said Arthur. Baz shoved the fossil into the back of the van, and they drove off, belching black fumes.

Naturally, Baz had to drive. Arthur looked back out of the window.

"Not too fast, Baz," he warned. "We want the ghost to follow us…"

And follow them it did. The poor ankylosaurus had no choice but to stay with its ankle, as all ghosts are tied to their bones or gravestones.

"*AAAOOOUUWWWRRROOOUUUGH!*"

After that, the Crabtrees returned to the cliff again and again, stealing fossil bones and luring away the dino-ghosts to whom the bones belonged. Arthur and Baz grinned their nasty grins, and Gilbert worried...

"What *are* they doing to those poor ghosts?"

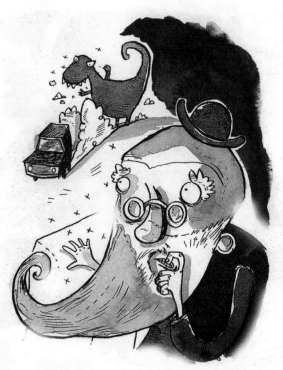

So the next time the brothers rolled up, and Baz began chipping away at the cliff, Gilbert sneaked into their van. He was looking for anything that might help him stop them.

On the front seat he found a laptop with a search engine on its screen. Gilbert had never seen a laptop before, but he was used to typewriters, so he tried typing *ghost* and *help*. His finger brushed the enter key. At the top of the page that appeared was:

www.ghostrescue.co.uk
Are you a ghost who's
getting grief...?

Quickly Gilbert typed a message for the mysterious Ghost Rescue, whoever *they* were... And some time later, after the Crabtrees had gone, he was puzzled to see an old pizza delivery van drive up.

Ghost Rescue climbed out of the Ghostmobile – first Charlie, then the ghosts of Lord and Lady Fairfax, their daughter Florence, Rio the parrot and Zanzibar the dog.

"How can we help?" asked Charlie.

The next day, Arthur and Baz's van appeared as usual. Once more Arthur gave the orders, once more Baz grumbled, and once more the cliff echoed to the *thwack-ack-ack* of Baz's pickaxe. Another great dino-fossil came loose.

"What kind of bone is that?" asked Charlie, from their hiding place.

"Looks like a stegosaurus skull," said Gilbert. "And...there is the stegosaurus!"

Zanzibar growled, and Rio squawked.

"Leaping lizards," gasped Lord Fairfax. "What a creature!"

"*AAOUUWWRROOUUGH!*" The great ghost of the stegosaurus stamped its feet, shook its bony spines, and roared with rage as Baz shoved its skull in the van.

The brothers drove off, with the poor ghost in angry pursuit.

"Another bone is stolen," sighed Gilbert. "Another poor dinosaur is kidnapped. It's always the same…"

"It's different this time," smiled Charlie. "*We're* here — and *we've* got wheels too."

Then Charlie chipped a piece off the memorial stone that reminded visitors of Gilbert's tragic accident, and put it in his bag with the Fairfax stone.

"All aboard the Ghostmobile," said Charlie. "Now you can come too, Gilbert!"

And off they drove, following the trail of thick black smoke from the Crabtree brothers' van.

Arthur and Baz drove to their ramshackle lock-up beneath a rotting bridge. The stegosaurus ghost roared and stamped, but the Crabtree brothers knew a ghost couldn't hurt them.

Baz picked up the stegosaurus's skull and shoved it inside a strange-looking steel box. Several large batteries were strapped to it.

"What sort of device is that?" asked Gilbert, as he and Ghost Rescue watched from the shadows.

"No idea," whispered four voices at once.

Arthur pulled out a remote control, and grinned at Baz. Charlie really didn't like the look of that grin.

Then Arthur and Baz loaded the steel box – skull and all – into the van, and drove off again. Ghost Rescue followed in the Ghostmobile, keeping out of sight.

Several miles later, the van reached the
grand estate of Foulfox Acres. Arthur and
Baz, or rather Baz, carried the steel box
through the gardens towards the mansion.
The stegosaurus ghost stamped along
behind, scaring the birds out of the trees.
Arthur spied a thick patch of nettles in
the shadow of the mansion wall.

"Right, Baz," said Arthur quietly, "you know what to do."

Baz grumbled as he carried the steel box over to the nettles.

"Why *me?*" he whispered. "Why do *I* have to go into the nettles?"

"Baz," hissed Arthur, "you *know* we have to hide the skull *exactly* where we want the ghost to be. And you *know* I'm allergic to nettles."

"Yes, Arthur, I know..." sighed Baz, as he heaved the device in among the stinging leaves.

"Ow!" said Baz. "I'm stung! Couldn't I at least have some gardening gloves?"

"*Baz*," hissed Arthur, "do you *know* how much gardening gloves cost?"

"Yes, Arthur," sighed Baz. "Sorry, Arthur…"

"Cheer up, Baz!" whispered Arthur. "It's all going according to plan. Just think of the money!" Arthur grinned, and even Baz, rubbing his sore hands, couldn't help smiling too…

"*AAOUUWWRROOUUGH!*"

"Lionel!" said Lady Foulfox as she and Lord Foulfox sat down to dinner in the mansion. "Was that you? I've *said* you need to see a doctor about your nervous wind—"

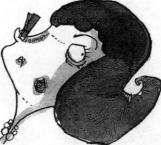

Just then, a ghostly dinosaur head loomed in at the window, and roared. "*AAOUUWWROOUUGH!*"

And Lord Lionel Foulfox really did
have something to be nervous about.
Thrrrrrp!

"*AAOUUWWRRAARRRRGH!*"

Foulfox Acres was in uproar. Maids and
butlers and groundsmen rushed about in
panic. At that moment, Arthur and Baz
drove up in their van. They had peeled
the paper off its sides, to show bold red
letters that read *Ghost Blasters*.

"Tumbling tombstones!" said Lord Fairfax. "What are they playing at now?"

Arthur and Baz stepped out of the van, quite unconcerned about the dinosaur ghost rampaging above their heads.

"Lady Foulfox, I presume?" said Arthur. "It seems you have a bit of a *problem*. It's a good thing we were in the area. Ghost Blasters can clear up this problem for you in no time at all. Perhaps we can step inside, and discuss our *fee...?*"

When Arthur named his price, Lord Foulfox had another nervous episode — *thrrrrrp!* But Lady Foulfox just sighed.

"I suppose we have no choice," she said coldly. "Very well, Mr Crabtree, it's a deal. Just get on with it."

Arthur began pretending to do all kinds of magical incantations. Then Baz, sitting out of sight in the back of the van, pressed a button on the remote control. Ghost Rescue were hidden in the nettles looking at the steel box, and watched as it crushed the stegosaurus's skull.

Crrr-rrrr-rrrrrunch!

The skull was crushed to powder.

"*AAOUUWWRROOUUGH!*" came the cry, louder and more terrible than ever before. Everyone in Foulfox Acres turned to look. The stegosaurus ghost howled, and shuddered, then faded away like smoke in a sudden breeze.

"*AAOUUWWRROOUUUUUUUUUUGH!*"

With a sigh of relief, Lady Foulfox paid the Ghost Blasters their fee — wads and wads of cash, which Arthur placed in a safe in the van. There was already a whole heap of money in there.

"Just the latest in a line of Ghost Blasting jobs, then," frowned Lady Fairfax, when Ghost Rescue were all back in the Ghostmobile.

"Nice work if you can get it," scowled Florence.

"Nice work if you can *create* it," added her father angrily.

"But what can we do to stop them?" said Charlie.

Charlie, Gilbert and the Fairfaxes put their heads together – and soon they had a plan...

The next day, Arthur and Baz visited the cliff again. They dug out the rib of a tyrannosaurus and took it to their van. The tyrannosaurus ghost stomped and shrieked and gnashed its terrible teeth in protest.

"AAAARRRRGHH-GARRRR-ARRRGH!"

Arthur and Baz opened the van and put the rib inside the crusher. Then they sat chatting and laughing in the front. They didn't notice Charlie creeping up to the back doors of the van...

"Locked!" whispered Charlie.

Lord Fairfax nodded. Quickly, he shrank in size and slipped into the lock, where he squeaked instructions for Charlie to open it.

Charlie sneaked into the back of the van and quietly closed the doors, just as Baz started the engine and pulled away.

The Ghost Blasters' next victims were Binkleford Bank. Baz took the crusher from the van, not noticing the small figure hiding under a tarpaulin. As Charlie crept away from the van, he saw Arthur make Baz climb down into the drains beneath the bank, clutching the crusher with the tyrannosaurus rib inside it.

"Ooh, it *stinks* down here!" wailed Baz. "Ugh, it's soaking up my legs... *Agh, a rat!*"

"Be brave, Baz," whispered Arthur. "Just think of the money!"

So Baz hid the crusher in the sludge and slime, and right above it the tyrannosaurus ghost stamped and snapped his terrible teeth.

"*AAAARRRRGHH-GARRRR-ARRRGH!*"

The customers of Binkleford Bank screamed, dropped their credit cards, and ran for their lives.

Just then – who would have guessed? –
the Ghost Blasters drove up.

"It seems you have a bit of a *problem*,"
Arthur said to the bank manager.

"Ghost Blasters can clear up this problem for you in no time at all. Perhaps we can step inside, and discuss our *fee…?*"

Arthur began pretending to do his spells and incantations. Baz was hiding in the van waiting to press the remote control and crush the tyrannosaurus rib to dust…when a boy came up to Arthur and the manager. He was just an ordinary boy, except that his shoes were slimy and smelly. Arthur didn't notice this. Perhaps he should have.

"Arthur Crabtree?" said the boy.

"What?" said Arthur, distracted from his spells. "Who are you?"

"Arthur Crabtree," said Charlie, "I need to warn you – *don't* use your remote control. Tell Baz not to press the button."

"*What?*" said Arthur, looking hard at Charlie.

"Remote control?" said the manager. "What's the kid talking about?"

"Oh, nothing!" smiled Arthur. "Just a crazy kid... Go on, shoo, kid! *Shoo!*"

Arthur chased Charlie out of the bank. Charlie ran to the Ghost Blasters' van, and opened the back doors. Baz was sitting inside, his finger hovering over the remote control. Baz didn't notice Charlie's smelly shoes either. Perhaps he should have.

"Hey!" said Baz. "Who are you?"

"It doesn't matter who I am," said Charlie. "I'm just warning you – don't press that button. Destroying these poor dino-ghosts is wrong. You must take the tyrannosaurus rib back to the cliff where it belongs."

Baz went very pale. "Who *are* you, kid?" he asked. "How do you know so much?"

"Don't listen to him!" snapped Arthur, who had followed Charlie. "The kid's bluffing. What does he know?" And Arthur pointed at the button, the button to crush the tyrannosaurus rib, to destroy the tyrannosaurus ghost, to save Binkleford Bank and earn Ghost Blasters another lovely fee...

"Press the button," said Arthur to Baz.

"I *strongly* advise you *not* to press it,"
said Charlie.

Arthur made a grab for the remote. "If
you don't press it, Baz, *I* will!"

"Please," said Charlie, "I beg you, *don't press the button!*"

But Arthur looked at Charlie with a horrible grin. "*Try and stop me!*" he sneered – and he pressed the button.

Arthur and Baz waited for the tyrannosaurus ghost to wither and die... But it didn't. There it was, still storming and raging.

"*AAAARRRRGHH-GARRRR-ARRRGH!*"

"What's going on?" said Arthur, and he pressed the button again and again.

The bank manager demanded to know *when* exactly they were going to do their jobs.

The Ghost Blasters spluttered some excuses, begged for a little more time, and scurried down into the drain to see what had gone wrong with the crusher.

"It's obviously malfunctioning," growled Arthur, as they crouched down in the slime beside the crusher, expecting to see the tyrannosaurus rib lying uncrushed inside.

It took a moment for their eyes to see in the darkness – but then they saw. They realised what had happened.

"*No...*" said Baz in a choking whisper.

"*Please, NOOO!*" howled Arthur.

There was nothing wrong with the crusher. When Arthur had pressed the button, it had done what it was told, and crushed what was inside.

Not a tyrannosaurus rib.

Their money.

All their lovely money – thousands and thousands of pounds of bank notes. It had been safely stashed in their safe in the van – and now it was all a crushed pile of papier-mâché.

"*NOOOOOOOOOOOOOO!*" shrieked Arthur, and the awful sound even scared the rats away. He pulled the mass of pulped money out of the crusher, and was desperately trying to pull the notes apart – when a torch shone down on him. It was the police chief, with the bank manager by his side.

"Destroying currency of the realm, eh?" said the police chief. "That's a criminal offence. You two had better come along to the station."

Arthur's and Baz's wails of protest were soon drowned out by the siren of the police van taking them to the station.

Meanwhile, a pizza delivery van drove quietly away. Inside the Ghostmobile, Charlie held onto the tyrannosaurus rib, which of course he had switched with the money after Lord Fairfax had helped him unlock the safe.

Everyone at Binkleford Bank was puzzled, but relieved, when the tyrannosaurus ghost suddenly stomped off, following the strange old van, following it all the way back to the cliff where he belonged...

"Thank you, Ghost Rescue," said Gilbert. "And thank you, Charlie – you're a real hero-saurus!"

WRITTEN BY
Andrew Murray

ILLUSTRATED BY
Sarah Horne

All priced at £3.99

The Ghost Rescue books are available from all good bookshops,
or can be ordered direct from the publisher:
Orchard Books, PO BOX 29, Douglas IM99 1BQ
Credit card orders please telephone 01624 836000
or fax 01624 837033 or visit our website: www.orchardbooks.co.uk
or email: bookshop@enterprise.net for details.

To order please quote title, author and ISBN
and your full name and address.
Cheques and postal orders should be made payable to 'Bookpost plc'.
Postage and packing is FREE within the UK
(overseas customers should add £1.00 per book).

Prices and availability are subject to change.